GOLDIE BLOX

AND THE BEST! PET! EVER!

For Suzanne and all dog lovers —S.M.

Visit us on the Web!
randomhousekids.com
GoldieBlox.com

Library of Congress Cataloging-in-Publication Data
McAnulty, Stacy.
Goldie Blox and the best! pet! ever! / written by Stacy McAnulty ;
illustrated by Alan Batson.
pages cm — (Goldie Blox and the Gearheads ; 3)
Summary: Goldie Blox enters her dog, Nacho,
in the Bloxtown Pet Talent Show.
ISBN 978-1-5247-1789-6 (trade) — ISBN 978-1-5247-1790-2 (lib. bdg.) —
ISBN 978-1-5247-1791-9 (ebook)
[1. Juvenile Fiction—Media Tie-In. 2. Juvenile Fiction—Humorous Stories.
3. Juvenile Fiction—Science & Technology.] I. Title.
PZ7.M47825255 Gnb 2017
[Fic]—dc23
2017001481

Printed in the United States of America
10 9 8 7 6 5 4 3 2
Random House Children's Books supports the First Amendment
and celebrates the right to read.

GOLDIE BLOX AND THE BEST! PET! EVER!

Written by Stacy McAnulty

Illustrated by Alan Batson and Grace Mills

Random House New York

PRESS THE MARSHMALLOW BUTTON

Goldie used her wrench to tighten one last hex nut. Then she jumped behind the steering wheel of her go-cart. She'd named it Blaze and had been working on it for weeks with the help of her best friends. The Gearheads, as she called them, had turned scrap metal and spare parts into a racing machine.

"Good luck, Goldie," Val Voltz cheered from the sidelines. "I'm going to close my eyes now. But I hope you win." She crossed her fingers and covered her face.

"You got this!" Li Zhang yelled. "There's no way you can lose. We added a second gas pedal and took away the brake. That go-cart is made for speed."

"What?!" Val turned white.

"Kidding," Li said.

Ruby Rails rolled her eyes. "Go get 'em, girl," she told Goldie.

"Thanks, Gearheads." Goldie put on her goggles. "I couldn't have done it without you."

As she turned the key and started Blaze, another go-cart pulled up next to hers. It was sleek and black and looked expensive.

"You haven't done anything yet," said the driver, Zeek Zander. "And I'm about to embarrass you in front of your friends."

Goldie revved the engine. "We'll see!"

A race marshal walked onto the platform carrying a green flag in his right hand. He reminded the contestants of the rules, like no bumping. Goldie was pretty sure that Zeek wasn't listening.

Then the marshal raised the flag. "On your mark. Get set."

Zeek's go-cart flew forward.

"Go!" The flag dropped.

Goldie mashed the gas pedal to the floor and gripped the steering wheel tight. She was right on Zeek's tail as they headed down the street. He looked over his shoulder. She waved.

Li had calculated that Blaze would finish the race in fourteen minutes and thirty-seven seconds. The record for the Bloxtown Go-Cart Race was fifteen minutes and three seconds.

Zeek and Goldie approached the first corner. Goldie eased off the gas. She knew this turn was tricky. Zeek's go-cart made it through easily. So did Goldie's. But two go-carts lost

control and sailed into a row of bushes.

They raced down another street filled with hills. As Blaze zoomed over a bump, Goldie's butt came off her seat.

"Wahooooo!" she yelled.

Zeek looked back again. She could see the shock on his face. They'd left all the other racers in the dust. But Goldie wasn't like the rest. She'd built her go-cart, and she'd practiced. She knew her chance to pass Zeek and take the lead was coming.

They raced up one street and down the next. People cheered and shouted along the sides of the road. Goldie would have waved her thanks, but she decided to save it for her victory lap.

When they got to Newton Avenue, Goldie swerved to the right side of the road. Blaze leaned hard on two wheels. She pressed the gas to the floor and darted by Zeek. She smiled, not caring if bugs flew into her mouth. The race was almost over, and she was in the lead.

They took the last turn. Goldie saw the finish line. She could imagine her mom and dad and the Gearheads waving banners. They'd go to the smoothie shop afterward to celebrate her victory. No, *their* victory.

But suddenly, something knocked into the back of Blaze. Zeek had bumped her. Blaze shook hard and weaved. Goldie straightened out her go-cart. But in that moment, Zeek passed her.

"It's not over yet. Come on, Blaze." Goldie shifted the go-cart into its fastest gear. Blaze rumbled as the tires spun.

Zeek and Goldie were neck and neck. This was it. She leaned forward in her seat as they flew across the finish line.

It was a tie!

Goldie held up her arms in victory. So did Zeek. Then she pressed the marshmallow button. A cannon on the back of the go-cart shot hundreds of mini-marshmallows into the air.

"Good race, Zeek," she said as their go-carts came to a stop.

"For me it was," he said. "I won."

Goldie caught a mini-marshmallow in her mouth. "It's a tie."

"No." Zeek shook his head. "Butler Phone! Show her." Zeek's state-of-the-art phone, which always hovered nearby, projected a picture for Goldie. It showed Zeek's go-cart winning by less than an inch.

"Oh. I guess you did win," Goldie said, shrugging.

"Why aren't you upset?" Zeek asked.

Goldie didn't get a chance to answer. She was surrounded by her friends and her parents. They high-fived and hugged.

"That was amazing," Ruby said. "We saw every second of it from my computer. Even Zeek's illegal bump." She gave him a hard stare.

"Goldie, you beat the record. You even beat my estimate by more than ten seconds. Totally awesome!" Li slapped her on the back.

"And I beat *her*!" Zeek stomped his foot like a two-year-old.

"We're proud of you," her mom said. "How about we get smoothies to celebrate? Dad and I will meet you at the car."

"To celebrate what?" Zeek demanded. "You lost."

"No," Goldie said. "We built an awesome go-cart and had an amazing race. It was so much fun!"

"Yeah," Val said. "You probably bought your go-cart online."

"Stop. I could beat you at anything. Anything!" Zeek pointed at a community bulletin board. "I could beat you at a 5K run or a chili cook-off."

"I prefer waffles," Goldie said.

Zeek kept pointing. "I could even beat you at the Bloxtown Pet Pageant."

"Do you even have a pet?" Val asked.

"Whatever," Zeek said. "I know I could beat

Goldie and her slobbery dog."

"No way!" Goldie yelled. "Nacho is the best." Her basset hound did slobber. A lot. It just meant he was really good at slobbering.

Zeek smiled. "I guess we'll have to see about that. Oh, and look at the prize." He read from the sign. "'The winner gets to name the new Bloxtown animal shelter.'"

"Really?" Li asked.

"I think I'll call it Zeek Zander's Home for Unwanted Pests."

Li ignored him. "G, we have to win this."

"Why? What's going on?" Ruby asked, looking confused.

"I want the new animal shelter named after my mom," Li explained. "I've been writing to the town council for months asking them to call it the Dr. Zhang Animal Shelter."

"Dr. Zhang was the greatest vet Bloxtown

ever had," Goldie said. "She did all the regular vet stuff, but she was also a famous scientist. She created new medicines and ways for pets to stay healthy. And she helped stray dogs and cats find homes."

"Wow," Val said.

"She was the one who brought me Nacho when he  was abandoned as a puppy. She just knew we belonged together."

"The town said they'd think about it. I really thought they'd name it after her." Li shook his head. "And now . . ."

"And now," Goldie said, "it will definitely be named after your mom. Because Nacho is going to win. I promise!"

Zeek laughed. "We'll just see about that."

MAYBE A BABY BONNET

The Gearheads celebrated their almost win at Frothy Formulas Smoothie Shop. But the entire time they sipped their drinks, Li didn't say a word.

"I think he's really worried," Val whispered to Goldie as they rode home.

"He doesn't need to be. Nacho is the best."

When they got to Goldie's house, they went right to her workshop. The BloxShop was Goldie's favorite place on earth.

"Nacho!" Goldie shouted. "We have news."

Nacho stopped licking his butt and looked

at her. He yawned and rolled onto his back, his tail thumping slowly.

"You're going to be a champion. You'll be named the best pet in Bloxtown."

Nacho farted. The noise scared him, and he jumped.

Val laughed. Ruby held her nose. And Li shook his head.

"What exactly does Nacho have to do to win?" Val asked.

"Ruby will find out," Goldie said.

"On it." Ruby took out her minicomputer to look up the pageant rules. "Okay. There are three categories that each pet must compete in. First, there's an obstacle course."

Goldie nodded. Nacho had never officially run through an obstacle course, but he lived in the Blox house, which was full of ladders and slides, secret passages and hidden tunnels.

"This will be easy, you'll see." Goldie grabbed a Hula-Hoop. "Nacho, jump through here, then crawl under that workbench. And circle the whiteboard three times after that."

Nacho wagged his tail but didn't move.

Li groaned. But Goldie wasn't discouraged.

"Hold this." She gave the hoop to Val, then grabbed a maple-flavored doggie treat from a box. That got Nacho's attention.

He sniffed the treat and followed it as Goldie pulled it away. She tried to lure him through the Hula-Hoop. He went around it. When she tried to get him to go under the workbench, he got stuck and she had to pull him out. And when she ran around the whiteboard three times, Nacho dropped out on the first lap.

"Is he napping?" Val asked.

"I think so," Goldie said. "We'll try again later. What else does he need to do?"

"The second part," Ruby continued, "is obedience."

"Like commands?" Goldie asked.

"Yes," Ruby said. "He needs to follow directions."

Goldie gave her a thumbs-up. Nacho could do that. Maybe. She placed the maple-flavored dog treat in front of his nose.

"Nacho," she said in a deep, clear voice that woke him up. "Eat." He gobbled up the treat right away. Goldie cheered and clapped.

"I don't think that's what they mean," Val said. "It's more like sit, stay, and roll over."

Goldie tilted her head and looked at her dog, who was now snoring. He could certainly fall asleep quickly.

"Nacho, sit."

Nacho didn't move.

"Nacho, speak."

Nothing.

"Nacho, lie down."

Nacho continued to sleep. Lying down.

"Good dog." She rubbed his back and kissed his head.

"Well, that was amazing," Val said.

"He needs his rest," Goldie said. "What else does Nacho have to do to win this thing?"

"The final category is talent," Ruby said.

"Nacho has oodles of talent. He's the most talented dog in Bloxtown. Maybe even the world." Goldie just couldn't think of anything off the top of her head.

"What talent does he have?" Val asked.

"Umm." Goldie scratched her chin. "It's not like he sings or dances or does gymnastics. But he's way talented."

"G, think about it." Li spoke for the first time since they'd left the go-cart race. "There are dogs that can help the blind and others that can find missing hikers. Nacho is only good at eating waffles really, really fast."

"Yes, he does eat waffles really, really fast. Maybe we'll do that as his talent." Goldie smiled at Li.

"Maybe we could dress

him up," Val suggested. "He looks really good in hats. Maybe a baby bonnet."

"Dressing up is not a talent," Li said.

"We'll think of something," Goldie said.

"Well, you better think fast. The pageant is next Saturday," Ruby said.

Li groaned.

"Are there any other rules?" Val asked.

Ruby looked down at her computer. "'The contest is open to any non-human member of the family, and only one entry per house is allowed. The winner gets to name the new Bloxtown animal shelter.' That's all. Should I register Nacho?"

"Yes!" Goldie answered.

Li collapsed onto a beanbag chair.

"We're going to win," Goldie told Li.

"I don't know, G. I love Nacho, but what if he can't beat Zeek? This is important."

"I know it is. And Nacho knows it, too." At least, she'd be sure to explain it to him when he woke up.

Li pushed himself off the beanbag. "I'm going home. I need to tell my grandfather."

"But—"

"I'll see you later." Li went out the BloxShop door. He didn't take the zip line that connected the two houses. Goldie and Li had been neighbors their whole lives. Goldie couldn't remember the last time Li left by going out the regular, old door.

"He's really feeling down," Val said. "If we don't win . . ."

"We will," Goldie assured her.

"And if Zeek wins—"

"He won't!" Goldie said. "It might not be easy. But we *will* win. We just need a plan."

A RUBY RAILS RED CARPET ORIGINAL

The next day after school, the Gearheads met at the BloxShop. Goldie stood at the whiteboard.

"Okay, Gearheads," she began. "We need a plan to make Nacho a winner!"

Nacho hurried over at the sound of his name. Val let him sit in her lap.

"Let's hear your best ideas," Goldie said.

"I have an idea for a costume," Ruby said. "It's the latest fashion and highly functional."

"Great." Goldie wrote Ruby's name next

to *talent* on the board. "What about you, Val? Maybe you can help with the obstacle course."

"No," Li said. "I'll do that."

"You will?" Goldie asked, hopeful. She was worried Li might not be up to helping.

"I was sketching some ideas during lunch. If Nacho is going to win, he'll need an epic obstacle course to practice on. Right?"

"I think he's just got to run around some cones and jump through a hoop," Val said. "What do you have in mind?"

"You'll see. It's not going to be like that one-person roller coaster I built last week. Try to imagine a ropes course and a carnival fun house mixed together." Li pulled out a tape measure and took Nacho's measurements.

"Sounds epic and a bit terrifying." Val shuddered. "I'll . . . um . . . give Nacho a bath and a belly rub. We need our champion well rested and groomed."

Nacho panicked when he heard the word *bath*. He jumped off Val's lap and tried to escape into the backyard. But Val grabbed him.

"Great. We got this!" Goldie slapped the cap on her marker.

"What about the commands? How's Nacho going to learn all the commands, like speak and heel?" Ruby asked.

"Don't worry, Ruby. I can engineer that." Goldie reached into her messy hair and pulled out a screwdriver. "Let's get to work!"

Li went outside to construct the obstacle course while Ruby set up at a desk in the corner. Val dragged Nacho into the house for a bath, and Goldie went to her workbench. She used parts from an old toaster, a not-so-old vacuum, and a broken computer. They each worked through the evening.

Finally, they finished as the sun was setting and it was almost time to go home.

"G, Val, Rubes!" Li yelled from outside. "Come check out my obstacle course."

The three friends ran into the backyard. Nacho chased behind them.

"Whoa!" Ruby said.

"Epic for sure!" Goldie exclaimed.

"That's not even possible," Val said.

They were staring at an obstacle course that was forty feet high and ran through both the Zhangs' and the Bloxes' backyards.

"Watch as I demonstrate," Li said.

"Can I try?" Goldie asked.

"Sure." Li handed her a helmet. "I've already done it a dozen times. I'll time you."

Goldie made her way to the starting line. She pushed up her sleeves and tightened her shoelaces. "Ready."

"I can't even . . ." Val seemed about to faint.

Li looked at his watch. "On your mark, get set, go!"

Goldie dashed across plastic lily pads and over a moat. No problem. Then she scaled a giant wall that was slick with cooking oil. It took a few tries.

"You're doing it!" Li yelled.

Next, she climbed a rope wall and walked across a twisting log that was ten feet off the ground. She stumbled, and Val screamed. But Goldie regained her balance and jumped onto the next platform.

"I wanted to add a river of fire to this part, but my grandfather said no," Li told them.

Goldie swung across the swaying rings.

"Only a bit harder than the ones on the playground," she yelled. The final obstacle was a trampoline. Goldie bounced and flew up to the second story, grabbing the crooked ladder and climbing to victory.

"I did it!" She took hold of the finisher's flag and waved it above her head.

Li whistled.

"Wahoo!" Ruby cheered.

"I'm so glad you're alive!" Val yelled.

Goldie rode the slide down to her friends and pushed her sweaty hair off her forehead.

"Li, that was awesome. How'd I do?" she asked, glancing at his watch.

Li smiled. "You beat my time. Okay, Nacho, it's your turn," he said, but Nacho was gone. "Where is he?"

"Do you really expect a basset hound to be able to do this obstacle course?" Val asked.

"If he can do this obstacle course, he can do any obstacle course," Li said.

"True," Goldie agreed. "But maybe

something smaller and less scary would work."

"He just needs to win," Li said.

"He will," Ruby said, stepping forward. "Wait until you see my creation." They followed her back inside the BloxShop. She found Nacho and told her friends that she needed just a second to get him dressed.

Goldie, Val, and Li sat on the couch.

"I hope she's come up with something amazing," Val said. "Because, um, the bath didn't go too well. I couldn't even get one paw in the tub."

"Almost ready." Ruby turned off the lights and used a flashlight. "Ladies and gentleman, Gearheads, I give you . . . the dapper Nacho."

Ruby paused. The three friends clapped. Nacho stepped into the spotlight.

"Snazzy!" Goldie said. The black tuxedo fit him perfectly.

"Nacho is wearing a Ruby Rails red carpet original design," Ruby explained. "Not only is this silk tux gorgeous, with gold buttons and a red bow tie, but it is also programmed to play music and stop shedding." Ruby tapped on her minicomputer and jazz music played from a speaker hidden in the collar of the tux. Nacho swung his head left and right, trying to figure out where the noise was coming from. When he realized it was emanating from somewhere near his neck, he began to scratch.

"What exactly is his talent?" Val asked. "Modeling, maybe?"

"No," Ruby said. She fiddled with her minicomputer and the music changed to country. "He's supposed to dance. There's even a subwoofer in the pants."

"A sub-what?" Val asked.

"A subwoofer. It vibrates with the bass," Ruby explained.

They watched the pants bounce with the low sounds in the music. But the subwoofer didn't make Nacho dance. Instead, he began chewing on his butt.

"No!" Ruby shouted.

Li turned on the lights, and Ruby and Goldie got the costume off the dog.

"Sorry, Ruby. I don't think he likes it much," Goldie said.

"The dog has no taste." Ruby looked angry until Nacho gave her a slobbery kiss. Then she laughed.

"This is not going well," Li said. "And we only have four more days." He pulled his hat down to cover his face.

"Wait until you see what I've come up with!" Goldie darted across the BloxShop. An old blanket covered her invention, which was taller than her. She lifted the corner and yanked back the blanket. "Ta-da!"

"What is it?" Val asked. "A toaster robot?"

"How can a toaster help?" Li asked.

"I call it the Commander," said Goldie, using her deepest voice. "It can give a hundred commands a minute. So while we're at school or sleeping, Nacho can continue to practice for the pageant." Goldie flicked an ON button.

Two glowing eyes lit up on the toaster face. The toaster moved forward toward the dog. Nacho whimpered and hid behind Val.

"Nacho, sit," the Commander ordered.

Nacho was already sitting.

"He did it!" Goldie exclaimed.

"Good dog," said the Commander. A waffle

flew out of the toaster's mouth.

Nacho caught the waffle in the air and swallowed it in two bites.

"Nacho, lie down," said the Commander.

Nacho didn't move. The Commander inched closer.

"Nacho, roll over."

Nacho still didn't move.

"Nacho, fetch."

"Nacho, heel."

"Nacho, speak."

Nacho did none of those things.

"Nacho, sit," said the Commander. And since Nacho was still sitting, the Commander said "good dog" and gave him another waffle.

"Um, Goldie," Val said after ten minutes. "I don't think this is working."

"We just started," Goldie said. "And Nacho already knows sit. Imagine how many commands he'll learn by the time we get home from school tomorrow."

Li shook his head. "I hope you're right, G. But maybe—"

"Don't worry. It'll be okay." She patted Li on the back, but Goldie was worried.

SOMETHING FURRY OR WITH FEATHERS

Goldie joined the Gearheads at their usual lunch table in HiBo Prep's cafeteria. She looked at her tray of spaghetti, salad, and a roll and wished she had some bacon bits to pour on top.

Li had a slice of pizza on his plate. But he wasn't eating.

"You okay?" Goldie asked him.

"The pet pageant is in three days," he mumbled. "I don't think Nacho will be ready."

"Don't give up, Li. I bet Nacho already

knows most of his commands." Goldie turned to Ruby. "Rubes, let's check in on our champion."

"Sure thing." Ruby tapped on her mini-computer. Her eyebrows scrunched together.

"What is it?" Goldie asked.

Ruby turned the minicomputer to show the Gearheads. "I don't think Nacho is listening to the Commander."

On-screen was a live video from the BloxShop. The Commander was yelling out commands. Nacho ignored the robot. He was too busy chasing his tail.

"I assume *catch your tail* is not one of the commands Nacho needs to learn," Val said.

"Nope." Goldie smiled and leaned closer to the screen. "But look on the bright side. When he wants something, he tries really hard and doesn't give up. He's been chasing his tail for

years and never, ever catches it."

"Ugghh." Li laid his head on the lunch table.

Goldie twirled spaghetti around her fork. She was a lot like Nacho. Never willing to give up, and also willing to work for waffles. But even Goldie worried sometimes.

Val offered to share her potato chips with Li. But he said he wasn't hungry. Ruby, Val, and Goldie ate in silence.

"Hey, losers," Zeek said as he walked by. His Butler Phone hovered behind him.

"Go away, Zeek," Ruby said.

"Wait," Goldie called out. "Zeek, how's the pageant prep going?"

"Amazing. I'm going to win." He looked at the ceiling as he talked, and Goldie thought he might not be telling the truth.

"Do you even have a pet yet?" Val asked.

"Yeah," Zeek answered.

"What kind?" Goldie asked.

"I don't remember." He shrugged.

Li raised his head. "You don't remember?"

"Yeah, I don't remember. Okay? Something furry or with feathers. Whatever it is, we're going to beat you and your dog." Zeek started to walk away, but Butler Phone began speaking.

"I remember, Master Zeek. We ordered a border collie, which is the smartest dog breed.

But it ran away."

"Stop," Zeek said.

But Butler Phone didn't hear or wasn't listening. "Next, we ordered a crow—a very smart bird. But it flew away. We considered a dolphin, an incredibly smart mammal, but Master Zeek finally decided on—"

"Butler Phone, quiet!" Zeek stomped his feet and turned red. "Don't tell them our winning strategy!"

"You can tell us, Butler Phone," Ruby said in her sweetest voice. "We're all friends."

"Not a word," Zeek warned. "Or I'll trade you in for a newer model."

"I'll say nothing more, Master Zeek." Butler Phone's glowing screen dimmed.

Zeek turned to Goldie. "I'll tell you this much. After I win, I'm going to name the animal shelter Flea Bag Hotel for Ugly Dogs, or maybe

I'll just call it Closed."

"But no one will ever go there," Val said.

"Exactly." He snapped his fingers and pointed. "Pets are disgusting. They go to the bathroom on the lawn and use their mouths to eat and clean. I think Bloxtown would be better off if it were animal free."

"What about companionship? And friendship?" Ruby asked.

"Get a Butler Phone. They're neat and clean. They listen. And if you get sick of them, just take out the battery."

"Sir?" Butler Phone gasped. "You'd never."

Li stood up quickly, knocking over his chair. "I can't take this anymore." He walked out of the cafeteria.

"What's his problem?" Zeek asked. "He

should be used to losing."

"You're trying to destroy something he cares about," Goldie said. "His mom was a vet, and the shelter should be named after her. She helped all kinds of animals."

Zeek rolled his eyes. "What a waste." He still didn't seem to care.

Now it was Goldie who turned red. "I'm not going to let you win! This is too important."

"You're not going to *let* me?" Zeek laughed. "You can't stop me."

Goldie balled her hands into fists. "I guess we'll find out this weekend."

"Whatever. Come on, Butler Phone. We've wasted enough time." Zeek walked away, but Butler Phone didn't follow immediately.

"I'm sorry, Miss Goldie," Butler Phone whispered. "I wish you the best of luck."

DOGGIE SEE, DOGGIE DO

After school, Goldie decided it was time to have a serious talk with Nacho. She sat him down on a stool in the BloxShop.

"Nacho, you're a good dog. The best dog! I wouldn't trade you for any other pet in the galaxy."

Nacho wagged his tail and Val asked, "Do you really think he understands you?"

"Mostly . . . I think." Goldie focused again on her dog. "Now I need you to prove to all of Bloxtown that you *are* the best pet. And it's not that hard. Watch."

Goldie stepped back and nodded at Val. They had a plan. They would teach Nacho by example. Doggie see, doggie do.

"Let's start, Val."

Val sighed. "Goldie, sit."

Immediately, Goldie sat on the ground.

"Good, Goldie." Val offered her a maple-flavored doggie treat.

Goldie pinched her nose. "I'd rather have those." She pointed to an open bag of gummy worms on her workbench. Val gave her a green one.

"Next command, please," Goldie said.

"Goldie, lie down."

Goldie lay down.

"See, Nacho? This is easy," Val said as she gave Goldie another gummy worm. "And it's yummy."

The girls practiced all the commands. Nacho watched them. They didn't stop until Goldie had a stomach full of gummy worms.

"I feel sick," she mumbled.

"Well," Val said. "I guess it's Nacho's turn."

"We'll do it together," Goldie suggested. She helped Nacho off the stool. They stood next to each other and stared at Val, waiting for a command.

"Sit," Val said.

Goldie sat. Nacho sat.

"Good dog." Goldie gave Nacho a hug, and Val gave him a doggie treat.

"Keep going," Goldie said.

"Roll over."

Goldie rolled over. Nacho yawned.

Val repeated the command. Goldie rolled over, but not Nacho. They tried again and again.

"I'm getting dizzy," Goldie said after the eighth time.

"Too bad you can't enter the contest," Val said. "You'd make a good pet."

"Let's give the obedience training a rest. We'll work on the obstacle course." Goldie opened the overstuffed cabinet in the corner of the BloxShop.

"How are you going to get a dog that doesn't know forward from backward to race through an obstacle course?" Val asked as she rubbed Nacho's head.

"I can engineer that!" Goldie exclaimed. She pulled out a helmet, a fishing vest, a remote control, and a broken toy helicopter. "This will just take a minute."

Val and Nacho barely had time to curl up on the beanbag and open a book before Goldie announced that she was done.

"Done with what?" Val asked.

"My latest invention." She held up a bulky vest and a helmet. "It's the Obstacle Aid. And I checked. It's not technically against the rules."

Goldie helped Nacho slip into the Obstacle Aid. She zipped up the vest and tightened the strap on the helmet.

"Let's try it out!" She ran to the backyard with Nacho by her side. Val came, too, but she wasn't as excited. They walked to the starting platform of Li's epic obstacle course.

"You're really going to let Nacho try this?" Val asked, wrapping Nacho in a protective hug.

"Yep," said Goldie, pulling a remote control out of her hair.

"You are a brave dog, Nacho," Val said.

Goldie counted down the start. "Three, two, one. Go, boy, go!"

Nacho took a tiny step onto a floating lily pad. His paws shook, and his tail trembled.

"Good job, Nacho." Goldie flipped a switch on the remote control, and suddenly she was driving Nacho through the course. The vest had springs that helped him jump from lily pad to lily pad. Ropes shot from the pockets and helped him cross the log. Hooks flew from the vest, and he swung easily across the ropes.

"Wow," Val said. "He's doing great. Are you sure this is allowed?"

"There's absolutely nothing in the rules against using an Obstacle Aid." Goldie fiddled with her remote some more. "And you haven't even seen the best part."

Suddenly, helicopter blades opened out of the top of the helmet. Nacho was flying! At

first, his feet kicked, and he howled. Then he relaxed. He seemed to like it.

Goldie continued to control the vest— and Nacho. She was determined to finish the obstacle course. But it seemed Nacho had other ideas. He chewed a few wires loose and clawed off the antenna.

"What's he doing?" Val asked.

"I don't know." Goldie banged the remote against her palm. It wasn't working.

Both girls stared straight up as Nacho flew over their heads. A tiny bit of drool dropped onto Goldie's forehead.

"Nacho, come down this instant." Goldie snapped her fingers.

"If you recall," Val said, "he isn't very good with commands."

The dog sailed across the backyard and through an open window of Goldie's house.

His tail was wagging the whole time.

"Come on. I know where he's heading." Goldie chased after him.

They found Nacho in the kitchen, raiding the highest cabinet. The helicopter blades whirled as he helped himself to cookies, cereal, and maple syrup.

"Nacho," Goldie said. "You'll get sick."

Nacho turned and gave her sad, puppy-dog

eyes. Then he flew down with a bag of oatmeal cookies in his mouth and dropped them in her hands.

"Aw, looks like he wants to share," Val said. "Such a sweet dog."

"Yes," Goldie said. "He is a sweet dog." *But he's not getting any closer to learning his commands or running the obstacle course,* she thought. "You're the best dog, Nacho. I just wish we knew what Zeek had planned."

"Well," said a voice from the open window. It was Li. "If you'd spent the afternoon spying on him like I did, you would know."

"And?"

"There's something you should see."

A GIANT WOODEN CRATE

Goldie had never said no to a spying mission. She put on her dark overalls, a black shirt, and a hat. Then she loaded a backpack with binoculars, rope, and snacks.

"I have to get home for dinner," Val said.

"Please come with us," Goldie begged.

"I'm still shaking from the last time," Val said, putting on her coat. "Let me know how it goes." She headed out the door.

"I guess it's just the three of us." Goldie nodded to Li and Nacho.

Outside, Li hopped on his hoverboard and Goldie rode her skateboard. Nacho, who was still wearing his vest and helmet, flew behind them. They raced through Bloxtown all the way to the Zander mansion.

A ten-foot-high wall surrounded the place. Cameras were posted on all the corners. A metal gate blocked the driveway. Goldie didn't see an easy way in.

"What are we looking for?" she asked Li as she jumped off her skateboard.

"I'm not sure, but a giant wooden crate was delivered to Zeek an hour ago. It said *Property of the Army* on the side." Li took a deep breath. "That can't be good."

Goldie looked up at Nacho, who flew nearby. "You can get over this wall the easiest. See what you can find out."

Nacho zoomed over the wall.

"How exactly is he going to tell us what he finds out, G?" Li asked.

"There's a video camera on the helmet," replied Goldie. "It's recording everything."

They stared up at the wall. Goldie paced back and forth. She wasn't good at waiting.

"Maybe I should have put on the doggie suit," she said.

"Or maybe you shouldn't spy!" A voice

behind Li and Goldie made them jump. Zeek had snuck up on them.

"We weren't spying," Goldie said. "We were playing Frisbee, and it went over your wall."

Zeek pointed to a security camera above them. "I've been watching the whole time. There's no Frisbee."

"What was in the big crate?" Li asked.

"You think I'm going to tell *you*?" Zeek sneered.

Li's shoulders dropped.

"Actually, I *am* going to tell you," Zeek said. "Because there's no way you're going to win the contest. Once you meet Ace, you can stop wasting your time on this pageant. If I were you, I wouldn't even show up."

"Oh, we're showing up," Goldie said. She

wouldn't know how to give up if she wanted to.

"Who's Ace?" Li asked.

"Follow me." Zeek walked them through the front gate.

"After we meet this Ace," Goldie whispered to Li, "maybe we can look for Nacho."

A large crate sat in front of the garage. One side of the box lay open, but Goldie couldn't see inside.

"Ace, come!" Zeek ordered.

A pair of glowing green eyes appeared from within the dark crate. Goldie and Li stared as a robot dog walked into the light and over to Zeek. The robot's head came up to Zeek's shoulder. Its body was silver and sleek. The tail was an antenna.

"That's Ace?" Li asked.

"That's your pet?" Goldie said.

"He's mine for the weekend. I'm renting

him from the army," Zeek explained. "He's super expensive, but I don't mind paying for perfection."

"That has *got* to be against the rules," Li complained.

"It's not," Zeek said. "My dad's lawyers checked. Do you want to see what he can do?"

"No," both Goldie and Li answered. But that didn't stop Zeek.

"Ace, sit. Jump. Lie down. Roll over. Beg. Heel." Zeek gave the basic commands, and Ace obeyed them. Then he gave harder commands.

"Ace, dig a four-foot hole."

Ace dug a perfect hole.

"Ace, climb that tree."

Ace climbed to the top of a birch.

"Ace, snap that flagpole in half."

Ace, with his huge jaw, did.

"He's . . . um . . . great," Goldie said. She

wanted to get out of there. "We'll just find Nacho and—"

"Ace can do that for you. Ace, fetch Nacho."

"No!" cried Goldie. But Ace was already gone.

"He's not going to eat Nacho, is he?" she worried.

"Or snap him in half?" Li added.

"No." Zeek laughed. "Not unless I order him to."

A few seconds later, Ace rounded the corner with Nacho riding on his back like a cowboy. He delivered the dog safely to Goldie.

"Thanks . . . I think," Goldie mumbled.

"We gotta go," Li said.

"Okay," Zeek said. "You probably have to get home and *not* enter the contest." He fell back laughing.

Goldie, Li, and Nacho walked out the gate.

"Maybe we shouldn't enter," Li said as he grabbed his hoverboard. "I don't want to be there when Zeek wins."

"No way. We're entering," Goldie said. "And if Zeek is entering a robot pet, we will, too."

Nacho growled. It was as if he understood what a robot pet meant for him.

"Don't worry, boy." Goldie scratched him behind the ears. "You'll always be my number one pet. But this is about winning. And getting to name the animal shelter."

"Where are we going to get a robot pet?" Li asked. "How are we going to afford it?"

"I can engineer it," said Goldie, jumping on her skateboard. "Come on. We're going to need Val and Ruby. Time to get to work."

HIP-HOP KITTY

Goldie stood at her workbench with her safety goggles securely in place.

"Wrench," she said.

Nacho wagged his tail and ran to the toolbox. He grabbed an adjustable wrench in his mouth and brought it to Goldie. She had to wipe off a bit of drool before she could use it.

Each of the Gearheads had a job. Ruby programmed the robot using her minicomputer. Val helped Goldie hold pieces in place. And Li calculated the force needed in the springs and mechanisms of their project.

"Flathead screwdriver," Goldie called out. Nacho got that for her, too.

They worked all day and through part of the night. But finally, the project was complete. Goldie slipped in a battery.

"Introducing eCat!"

eCat opened her huge eyes and yawned. Nacho sniffed her from head to tail. eCat growled and took a swipe at him.

Nacho yelped and backed away from the mean robot. Val gave him a doggie treat. He took it back to his bed. Alone.

"None of that," Goldie said, picking up eCat and placing her on the floor.

"Let's try her out," Li said.

"Go ahead," Goldie told Li.

Li stood in front of eCat and said, "eCat, run in circles seventeen times."

The robot cat started racing around Li's ankles.

"Geez, most people would start with something simple like sit," Val said.

"Simple isn't going to win," said Li as he watched eCat go around and around.

"Is anyone counting?" Ruby asked.

"I bet eCat is," Goldie said proudly.

After eCat finished her laps, Li gave more commands. Some were normal, like lie down. Others were crazy: hang upside-down like a possum. eCat did them all perfectly.

"Time for the obstacle course!" Goldie shouted.

The Gearheads and eCat walked toward the door. Nacho whimpered. They were all leaving him. Even Val.

eCat raced through the obstacle course. The robot made it look easy. She bounced, ran,

swung, and leaped without making a single wrong move.

"Wow! eCat beat my time," Li said. "We might actually win this thing after all."

Nacho watched from the window as Goldie and her friends surrounded eCat. They smiled and high-fived. Nacho whimpered.

When they came back inside, Ruby was suggesting ideas for the talent portion. "With a few small changes to the program, I think I can have eCat rapping songs in no time. We can have a hip-hop kitty."

"That's a great idea, Rubes," Goldie said. "Let's do it. And I want to add suction cups to her back paws. I think eCat will be able to scale walls even faster."

"I have some at my house," Li said. "Be right back." He grabbed the zip line and swung out the window.

Nacho walked over to Val. He rubbed against her leg, then rolled onto his back, looking for a belly rub.

"eCat could use a treat," Val said, ignoring him. "Maybe some grease for her joints. We don't want our star getting stiff."

"This might be our best invention ever. We rock!" Goldie said.

"eCat rocks!" Ruby added.

This time, while the Gearheads worked on improving eCat, Nacho didn't help. Instead, he stole eCat's battery and hid it. But Goldie quickly found it.

"How did eCat's battery end up in a shoe?" she asked.

"No idea," Ruby answered.

"Bet I could guess," Val said, staring at Nacho.

Nacho dropped his head and slinked off to his doggie bed.

While the Gearheads took a snack break, Nacho lured eCat away with a piece of string. She followed, and Nacho trapped her inside a laundry basket. But a laundry basket didn't make a good cage for an animal as smart and well-equipped as eCat. She found her way out in seconds.

Then Nacho accidentally-on-purpose knocked eCat out an open window. But eCat landed gracefully on her feet.

"eCat, get inside. We need you!" Goldie yelled. "And it's about to rain. You can't get wet. You'll be ruined."

"I guess I won't be giving her a bath," Val said.

"No baths for eCat. She can't get wet at all," Goldie explained.

A few minutes later, Nacho walked into the BloxShop carrying a pail of water in his mouth. He went straight for eCat. Maybe he hadn't heard Goldie's warning, or understood it. Or he totally had heard and understood.

"No!" Goldie shouted before Nacho could dump the bucket of water over eCat. "Nacho, stop. Bad dog! You know how important it is that we win this pageant. You could ruin everything."

Nacho set down the bucket. Not a drop spilled. Then he tucked his tail between his legs.

"Goldie, you're being harsh," Val said. "I'm sure Nacho doesn't want to ruin anything."

"I know." Goldie petted his head. "Why don't you just take a nap? We don't need you right now."

Nacho crawled back to his doggie bed. He buried his head under his paws. He whimpered. But no one gave him any attention or tried to make him feel better. The Gearheads were too busy fussing over eCat.

Li returned with the suction cups. Val polished and greased the robot. Ruby worked on the program. And Goldie put it all together.

They rebooted eCat and she worked even better than before.

"eCat is the best. She is so going to win!" Goldie said.

"And we'll get to name the animal shelter after my mom." Li smiled for the first time all week.

They huddled over eCat and put their hands in for a cheer.

"On the count of three, say hip-hip-hooray for eCat," Goldie said. "One. Two."

Nacho left the BloxShop before the count of three. No one noticed.

DOGNAPPED BY ALIENS

That evening, Goldie brushed her teeth, then went to her room and climbed into bed. eCat was lying on a pillow, and Nacho was curled up on the floor.

There was a knock on the door, and her parents came in to say good night.

"Big day tomorrow," said Goldie's dad, kissing her forehead.

"Yep, and we're ready." Goldie patted eCat on the head.

"I'm sure you'll do your best," her mom

said. "You always do."

"Thanks, Mom." Goldie gave her a hug.

"Just like I'm sure Nacho has been trying to do his best, too." Goldie's mom gave Nacho a doggie treat from her pocket and scratched him under his chin.

"Good night, Goldie," said her parents, and they walked out of the room.

Goldie closed her eyes. She fell asleep quickly with a big smile on her face. She dreamed of eCat winning the pageant and Li doing a victory dance. In her dream, he danced like a crazy chicken.

The next morning, Goldie woke with a gushy, sick feeling in her stomach. She bolted up in bed. She knew something was wrong. But she didn't know what.

At first, she thought she'd overslept and missed the pageant. But she looked at the

clock, and it was hours before they needed to be at the town hall.

Then she thought about eCat. Goldie found her lying still next to her. eCat was in the exact same spot she'd been last night.

Must be my imagination, Goldie thought.

She hit her bed's ejection mechanism and flew into her waiting overalls.

"Time to get up, Nacho," she said as she

fastened the buttons. "I'm in the mood for spicy, cheesy waffles."

Usually, Nacho was in the mood for waffles, too—or any food. But he wasn't racing toward the door like he normally did.

"Nacho?"

He wasn't in his bed. Or under her desk. He wasn't in her room at all.

Goldie ran, swung, climbed, and jumped through the entire house calling Nacho's name. It was useless. He was gone.

"Calm down, Goldie." Her dad made her sit in a kitchen chair. "We'll find him."

"I've called your friends," her mom said. "They'll be here any minute." The Gearheads showed up two minutes later. But to Goldie, it felt as if Nacho had been gone for days.

They all gathered around the table.

"What could have happened?" Li asked. "Do

you think he was dognapped by aliens?"

"No," Ruby said. "Stop talking crazy."

"Well, someone must have dognapped him," Goldie said, biting her lip to keep from crying.

"Or he ran away," Val mumbled.

"Why would he run away?" Goldie asked.

Val shrugged. "Maybe he feels unwanted. Like he was being replaced." She looked at eCat, who was standing perfectly still in the kitchen doorway.

"He's totally wanted," Goldie replied. "I just wanted to win the contest, too."

Li slumped into a chair. "And you were doing it for me, G. This is all my fault."

"No." Goldie shook her head. "This is on me."

Goldie felt awful. She would give away everything she owned to save Nacho. She'd say goodbye to her favorite overalls, her tape

75

measure, all her tools, and even the BloxShop. Nothing was more important than her parents, her friends, and Nacho.

"I messed up. But we'll find him," she said.

"Yes, we will," Ruby said, tapping on her minicomputer. "And I'm one step ahead of you. I've sent out a drone with a camera to check out all of Nacho's favorite places."

"Where did you get a drone?" Val asked.

"I may have borrowed one from HiBo Prep. And I may have hacked the system. And I may need you to keep this a secret."

They huddled around the screen.

"Try Frothy Formulas," Val suggested.

Ruby controlled the drone on her keyboard. On-screen, they saw the smoothie shop come into focus.

"Is he there?" Val asked.

The drone circled the building and peered

in the windows.

"No," Ruby said.

"How about the Galaxy Diner? Nacho loves their bacon-flavored ice-cream," Li said.

The drone checked it out. No Nacho there.

Ruby flew the drone over the deli, the grocery store, the bakery, and the pizza parlor. There was no sign of Nacho.

"Where could he be?" Ruby asked. "There's nothing Nacho loves more than food."

"Yes, there is," Goldie said. "Us. And I know where he is. Let's go."

"You don't want to use the drone?" Ruby said, but Goldie was already running out the front door.

Li took his hoverboard. Goldie rode her skateboard. And Ruby and Val shared a two-seater bike that was fitted with rocket boosters.

"You promise you won't use those, right?"

Val asked Ruby as they rode down the street.

Goldie led the way. She took every corner at top speed and went downhill so fast her hair flew straight back.

"We might need them if Goldie goes any faster," Ruby shouted to Val.

"I can't watch." Val left the driving up to Ruby.

"Where are we going, G?" Li yelled.

"There!" Goldie pointed to a building.

A few seconds later, they were in front of the town hall. They jumped off their vehicles.

"This is where the pageant will be held in a few hours," Val said. "You think he's in here?"

"Yep. Come on." Goldie ran around to the back of the building, where the obstacle course was set up. And just as she'd thought, Nacho was there. They watched as he tried to jump over the hurdles, run around the cones, and cross the balance beam. When he stumbled, he got back up and tried again.

"He refuses to give up," Val said.

"Reminds me of someone I know." Li elbowed Goldie.

Finally, Nacho crossed the finish line. The Gearheads cheered and shouted, "Nacho! Nacho! Nacho!"

The dog jumped in surprise. But when he saw who they were, his tail wagged with excitement.

Goldie ran over to him and wrapped him in a big hug.

"I was so worried," she said. "And I'm sorry. You're the best pet in all of Bloxtown, and I want you to enter the pageant."

Nacho licked her cheek.

"I have an idea." Goldie stood up. "Li, you can enter the pet pageant, too. With eCat."

"Good thinking, G," Li said. He patted Nacho on the head. "Let's do it."

ACE ACES EVERYTHING

The Gearheads burst into the kitchen of the Blox house. Goldie's dad looked up from the table where he was fixing a hairdryer.

"You found Nacho." He smiled.

"Yep. Now we only have an hour before we need to get to the pageant," Goldie said.

"I'll grab Nacho's costume," Ruby said. "I left it in the BloxShop."

"Come on, Nacho, I'll brush your teeth," Val said.

Nacho froze in his tracks.

"After I give you a yummy treat first, of course." Val opened the cabinet that contained doggie snacks.

"And I'll get eCat," Li said.

"eCat?" Goldie's dad said, rubbing his chin. "You need eCat?"

"Yeah," Li said.

"Sorry, kids." Goldie's dad stood up. "I disassembled her. I needed the battery back for my electric razor, and I needed the motor back in the Weedwacker. I didn't realize she was still part of your plan."

Li's shoulders slumped. "It's okay, Mr. Blox. eCat wasn't a real pet."

Goldie kneeled down in front of Nacho. "You're a true pet, Nacho. You're part of this family."

"And you're a Gearhead," Val added.

Goldie stared at her dog. "I still think you can win this."

"It's all up to you, boy," Li said.

Goldie hugged Nacho. "Just try your best."

Goldie couldn't believe how many pets were entered in the pageant. People brought dogs, cats, snakes, parrots, lizards, and mice.

But there was only one robot—Ace.

"Zeek and Ace are up next on the obstacle course," Goldie said, pointing at the schedule. "Let's go watch."

But in the minute it took them to walk outside, they were too late. Ace had already completed the obstacle course. He did it perfectly and in record time. The judges were taking selfies with the *amazing* Ace.

"Did you miss that?" Zeek rubbed Ace's victory in their faces. "Anyone who blinked missed it, really. You still have time to watch us in the obedience competition."

Zeek called Ace over, and they walked toward the gym.

"I don't want to watch," Goldie moaned. "But I also want to watch."

"Let's go," Ruby said. "I like to size up the competition."

The Gearheads, including Nacho, took a seat on the bleachers. Zeek and Ace stood in the middle of the gymnasium. A list of the commands was written on a board.

Zeek spoke. Ace obeyed. They got another perfect score. Some people in the stands even threw flowers at their feet.

"Good for them," Goldie said, trying to mean it.

"Ace is perfect," Val said, nibbling leftover waffles. "Even his name is perfect. Ace aces everything."

Zeek looked over at the Gearheads and gave them a little wave.

"It's almost Nacho's turn. We should head to the obstacle course," Goldie said. She wanted to get out of there before Zeek tried to taunt them even more. But as they hurried down the bleachers, they were stopped by Butler Phone.

"I have a message from Master Zeek," it said. Then Butler Phone played a recorded memo. "Hello, Goldie and her loser friends. I've been thinking about a name for the animal shelter. I can't decide between Useless and Pathetic. I mean, why would anyone adopt a disgusting animal when they could have a pet like Ace?"

"Message received," Ruby said. "Now go away."

"But there's more," Butler Phone said, and he continued playing the memo. "Maybe instead of naming the shelter, I'll just close it down. They'll let me do that. My dad *is* the mayor. We'll be one step closer to a clean, smart, animal-free Bloxtown."

"Can you record a message from us?" asked Ruby, grabbing the hovering phone.

"Don't hurt me," Butler Phone squealed.

"It's okay, Rubes," Goldie said. "Let it go. We can still win."

"Fine." Ruby let go of the phone, and it flew off toward its owner.

Goldie led them down the bleachers, out of the gym, through the crowded hall, and to the check-in table. Nacho happily followed because Val had a pocket full of waffle pieces that she kept dropping.

As they stood in line, Goldie grabbed Li's arm and pulled him aside.

"I don't know if Nacho can beat Ace, the wonder robot dog." Goldie wanted Li to be ready in case the worst happened.

"I know, G. It's like asking a horse to beat a car or a bird to beat a plane. He'll do his best." Li took a deep breath. "And I know my mom would have been proud of both Nacho and you. He's a good dog, and you're a good friend.

The best."

Goldie slugged him in the arm. "Don't get all mushy on me, Li Gravity. At least, not yet. You can save it for the end when we win this thing."

"But you just said—"

"Whatever. Don't distract me."

"Okay."

"Nacho is going to do great in the obstacle course," Goldie said.

"How?"

Goldie pulled her idea notebook from her pocket and a pencil from her hair. "I can engineer that!"

EATING? NAPPING? SLOBBERING?

After drawing up her plans, Goldie explained her idea to the Gearheads.

"We don't have much time. Val, I need you to snap a photo of the waffles you're eating."

"There's not much left, but okay," Val said.

"Ruby," Goldie continued, "can you turn your minicomputer into a hologram machine? You only have about five minutes."

"I only need two," said Ruby, pulling out her computer and getting to work.

"Li, I need to get over the obstacle course.

Nacho's helicopter helmet can't lift me. So I came up with this." Goldie showed Li her design with ropes, levers, and pulleys. "I just need something to attach it to."

"The flagpole," Li suggested.

"I bet they have most of what we need in the storage closet." Goldie smiled. "And I promise we'll put it all back when we're done."

Li ran to get supplies. Val took a picture with her cell phone and uploaded it to Ruby's computer. Ruby projected a hologram of a waffle with butter, syrup, and sprinkles.

"I added the toppings," she explained. "I thought Nacho might like it."

"I think he does." Goldie pointed at Nacho, who was licking his lips.

"Will Nacho Blox report to the starting line," a voice boomed over the loudspeaker.

Val and Ruby took Nacho. Goldie borrowed

the minicomputer and went to find Li, who was putting the finishing touches on the contraption.

"I didn't have time to test it," he warned her.

"No sweat." Goldie got into the harness. Li pulled the rope, and Goldie flew over the obstacle course.

"Ready!" she shouted to Ruby and Val.

"On your mark, get set, go!" said the judge.

Goldie turned on the minicomputer and the waffle hologram. She projected the image onto the obstacle course. Nacho ran straight for it.

"It's working!"

Li moved Goldie. Goldie moved the hologram. And Nacho raced through the obstacle course, finishing with the second-best time of the day.

Ruby and Val met him at the finish line. Val gave him a real waffle.

"Way to go, Nacho!" Goldie cheered.

Li helped her down. She high-fived him.

"We still have a chance," she said.

Next up was the obedience competition. Li and Goldie joined Val, Ruby, and Nacho outside.

"Do you have a plan?" Val asked.

"Absolutely." Goldie pulled out her notebook. "We're going to make some changes to Ruby's tuxedo."

"We are?" Ruby asked. "You're not talking about adding polka dots, right? Because polka dots are out this season."

"Nope," Goldie said as Val pulled the tux from a bag. "I want you to add some vibrating buttons." Goldie marked the spots where she wanted the buttons sewn in.

"And we need to work them remotely," she continued.

"On it!" Li said.

They got to work and had the new and improved outfit ready in no time.

Val picked up the tuxedo. "Is it going to give Nacho a massage?"

"Nope. It's going to tickle him. I call it the Tickle Tux." Goldie pointed to one of the hidden buttons. "You see—"

"G, you don't have time to explain. Nacho is up," Li said.

Ruby helped the dog get dressed and then Goldie and Nacho ran to the center of the gym. The crowd giggled at the well-dressed pooch.

The judge told them to perform the commands written on the whiteboard.

"You ready, Nacho?" Goldie whispered to

her dog. He looked up at her with his big eyes. She knew he'd do his best.

"Sit, Nacho." And he did. That was the one command he knew well.

"Stay, Nacho." She held up her hand and walked away. He started to follow, so she said it again. This time he stayed.

"Good dog! Now speak!"

Nacho didn't move. Goldie nodded at Li. It was time for the Tickle Tux to help out. Li flipped a switch that made the hidden button sewn into the bow tie vibrate.

Nacho barked.

"Good dog!" Goldie stepped closer and rubbed his fluffy head. Then she told him to lie down, and Li used the remote to activate the buttons on the belly of the tux. Nacho dropped to the floor.

It's working, Goldie thought.

Nacho finished the contest. He did all the commands. Some took two or three tries. But eventually, he got them.

"Well done," one of the judges said. "And I like Nacho's tuxedo. Very handsome."

"It wasn't just for looks," Goldie admitted. "We sewed in tickle buttons to help him learn his commands. Hope that's okay."

"It's genius," the judge said. "And well within the rules."

"Thanks."

The Gearheads waited patiently for Nacho's score. They watched another judge write it on a piece of paper and raise it over her head.

"I'm so nervous. I can't look." Val put her hands over her eyes.

"You can look," Ruby said. "He got a nine!"

"That's the third-highest score behind Zeek and a parrot!" Li cried.

"And our best is yet to come," Goldie said.

"What's Nacho doing for his talent?" Val asked. "Eating? Napping? Slobbering?"

"He's good at all those things." Goldie laughed. "But he's going to do what he does best. Help me."

Suddenly, Zeek shoved his way into their circle. "Not bad for a simple dog," he said. "But you still aren't going to win."

Goldie wasn't certain, but she thought Zeek sounded a bit nervous.

"We'll just have to wait and see," she said.

"You better hurry. Nacho is onstage next," Zeek said. "I needed to recharge Ace, so I had the judges change the order. Good luck. But I don't mean that."

An announcement came over the loudspeaker. "Nacho Blox, report to the main stage now!"

Goldie and Nacho ran to the theater and onto the stage. The rest of the Gearheads sat in the second row, right behind the three judges.

"I need two seconds," Goldie explained. She dragged a table to the center and laid out broken odds and ends on top of it. Then she put her toolbox near the stage door.

"How about some music, Rubes," Goldie called to her friend.

"You got it." Ruby used her minicomputer to fill the room with rock music.

Goldie picked up a belt and a wheel. Then she looked at her dog.

"Screwdriver," she said.

Nacho bolted across the stage to the toolbox. He pulled out a red-handled screwdriver and brought it back to Goldie.

"Thanks," she said, wiping off his slobber. "Hammer."

Nacho found the hammer and delivered it to Goldie. They did this again and again as the music thumped. Goldie tinkered, and Nacho fetched tools. The crowd watched with their heads bobbing along to the music.

"One last adjustment," Goldie said. She sent Nacho for a wrench and more nuts and screws. She tightened a final bolt.

"And voilà!" she said, setting the invention in the front of the stage and nodding for Ruby to cut the music.

The crowd murmured, and Goldie knew they weren't sure what exactly they were looking at.

"It's a Treadaffler!" she explained. "It's a waffle maker powered by a treadmill."

Goldie poured some waffle batter into the back of the contraption. "You can make waffles when the power goes out or while camping. My dog, Nacho, will demonstrate."

Goldie pointed to the platform, and Nacho jumped on. He started to jog, and the machine lit up.

"It takes about three minutes," Goldie said. "Keep going, boy."

Nacho ran for three minutes. His tongue hung out of his month. The Treadaffler rang and a waffle flew out like a Frisbee. Nacho caught it in his jaws. He hopped off the Treadaffler and began to munch.

Everyone clapped and jumped to their feet. Goldie looked at the judges. They held up three scorecards: 10! 10! 10!

OPERATION WIPEOUT

Goldie and Nacho bowed. Then they joined the Gearheads in the audience.

"That was great," Val said, hugging Goldie and kissing the top of Nacho's head.

"Look!" Li pointed at the scoreboard. "Nacho's in the lead."

"Yeah," Ruby said. "But Zeek and Ace still have to perform."

"And that parrot," Val added.

"Well, Nacho did his best. We'll just wait and see." Goldie smiled. "Or we could go wish

Zeek good luck."

They found Ace and Zeek standing by the stage steps. Butler Phone hovered nearby.

"Break a leg, Ace," Goldie said. She didn't actually mean for the robot to get hurt.

"What is Ace doing for a talent?" Li asked.

"He's winning, that's what he's doing." Zeek's face was red and sweaty.

"Ace will be reciting Shakespeare," Butler Phone answered.

"No!" Zeek snapped. "That's what he *was* going to do. We've got something even better."

"We do, Master Zeek?"

Zeek turned his back on the Gearheads and whispered to Butler Phone. Goldie slid closer so she could hear.

"We need something grand and legendary. Crack the code! Find out the hardest thing that Ace can do."

"Yes, Master Zeek."

A judge called Ace onto the stage. Zeek looked over his shoulder at Goldie. "Be ready to lose."

Ace and Zeek walked to the center of the stage. The audience and judges leaned forward in their seats. Butler Phone stayed in the shadows.

Li rocked back and forth on his feet. Goldie had never seen her friend nervous before. Not even when they'd invented the world's largest skateboard ramp. She wanted to tell him that it would be okay, but she didn't know that for sure.

The robot dog sat. Zeek stood.

"You may begin," a judge said.

"Um," Zeek muttered. Then he turned to Butler Phone and gave a mean stare.

"Your master looks mad," Goldie said.

"Oh dear," Butler Phone said. "I've almost got it." The phone screen flashed with code.

"We're not exactly rooting for you," Val said.

"Got it!" Butler Phone flew out onto the stage and whispered in Zeek's ear.

An evil smile spread across Zeek's face. He looked down at his robot dog.

"Ace, begin Operation Wipeout!"

Ace's eyes changed from a green glow to red. He stood up and started barking and snarling. Zeek stepped away from his robot pet.

"What's happening?" Goldie asked. "Ace is going crazy."

"I don't know," Ruby said. "I'll try to find out." She tapped on her minicomputer.

Ace jumped off the stage and chased down the other animals. Then he ran after the judges

and the audience. Every person and pet jumped to their feet and started to run.

"Bad robot dog!" Zeek yelled.

Ace turned and locked his eyes on Zeek.

"We have to help." Goldie raced toward Zeek, but Ace had him cornered.

"Butler Phone, turn Ace off!" Zeek yelled.

"I don't know how, sir." Butler Phone flew toward the exit. "But as soon as I'm safely outside, I'll begin researching that."

"Do something, please!" Zeek begged Goldie and her friends. They were the only ones who hadn't run off.

"Ace, sit!" Goldie said. She knew the robot dog was usually very good with commands.

But Ace didn't sit. Instead, he swung his head and growled at her.

"Ruby, have you found anything?" Li asked.

"You better hurry," Val said. "Before Goldie

becomes a robot chew toy."

"This is all I found." Ruby read from her minicomputer. "'Operation Wipeout is a command used to evacuate a building in case of an emergency.' Ace is just trying to get everyone to safety."

"But how do we shut him down?" Goldie asked. She stood still, trying not to draw any more attention from Ace.

"We just have to say the secret command," Ruby explained. "Which I'm trying to find. They don't just post secret commands online."

"Maybe he has an OFF button," Goldie said. "If we can just get close enough."

"If you get any closer, he might bite your leg off," Val warned.

"Good point."

"I have an idea." Li grabbed his hoverboard

and rode it in front of Ace. The robot dog snapped its powerful jaws but missed.

"Is your idea to get eaten?" Val yelled.

Nacho whimpered and shook.

Ace chased Li on the hoverboard. That gave Zeek a chance to escape.

"See ya," he said as he ran out.

Ruby continued searching for the secret OFF command. Goldie grabbed a hoop, a broom, a mop, and a tutu and engineered a giant telescoping net.

"Look for the OFF button. There has to be one." Goldie handed Val a pair of binoculars.

"Li," Goldie called out. "Get him back onstage." She held out her net, ready to capture the robot dog.

"I'm heading your way!" Li yelled to Goldie.

He zoomed across the stage. Ace followed close behind. Goldie ejected her net, but she missed. Ace turned and growled. His metal teeth gleamed under the lights.

Goldie stepped back and tried to reload her net. Ace moved in her direction.

Out of nowhere, Nacho leaped between them. He barked like a mad dog. He was louder and angrier than Goldie had ever heard him. But Ace kept moving toward him and Goldie.

Goldie put a hand on Nacho's head. She

needed to say something before they were both destroyed by a crazed robot. She didn't have much time.

"Nacho," she began, her breath catching. "What would I do without you? You're such a good dog." And just like that, Ace stopped snarling and sat.

Operation Wipeout was over.

"What happened?" Goldie asked.

"You did it!" Ruby joined Goldie onstage and read from her minicomputer. "'Say 'good dog' to stop Operation Wipeout.'"

Ace wagged his tail. His red eyes changed back to green.

"Seems harmless now," Val said with a nervous laugh. "But I think I'll still turn him off." She flipped the switch on the robot's belly.

"There's only one good dog here." Goldie squeezed Nacho as tight as she could.

AND THE WINNER IS . . .

The judges decided to continue the pageant even after Ace chased away most of the contestants. Goldie, Nacho, and the Gearheads waited outside as the final pets finished. They watched as Zeek tried to get Butler Phone to enter as a pet.

"It's not too late," Zeek said.

"Master Zeek, I keep telling you. I'm not a pet. I'm state-of-the-art technology." Butler Phone hovered just out of Zeek's reach.

"Well, today you are a pet. A robot pigeon." Zeek was turning red.

"A pigeon? No, Master Zeek."

"I don't think Zeek is going to win this argument," Ruby said.

"Who knew a phone could grow a backbone," Val joked.

A crackle on the intercom interrupted Zeek and Butler Phone's argument. It was time to announce the winner.

All the contestants gathered onstage for the awards ceremony. Goldie and Nacho were near the edge. The leader board was no longer there. Ace had smashed it to pieces during Operation Wipeout.

Ace, of course, had been disqualified.

A judge stood with a microphone in the center of the stage. "Thank you all for entering the Bloxtown Pet Pageant. As you know, the winner will get to name the new animal shelter. That's quite an honor."

Goldie flashed the Gearheads a smile.

"And the winner is . . ." The judge opened an envelope. "It's a tie. Chirper the parrot with her owner, Mrs. Friedman, and Nacho the dog with his owner, Goldie Blox!"

The Gearheads jumped to their feet, clapping and whistling. Goldie hugged her dog.

Chipper and Mrs. Friedman stepped forward, as did Goldie and Nacho. Another judge handed them a huge trophy. Goldie and Mrs. Friedman held it high in the air.

"In addition, we have a special award to give out," the judge said. "To Nacho and Goldie for saving the day." He hung a medal around Nacho's neck that read *Hero*.

The Gearheads rushed to the stage.

"Who gets to name the shelter?" Goldie

asked excitedly.

Mrs. Friedman turned to her. "Well, since you won two awards, you can name the shelter, my dear."

"Thank you." Goldie shook her hand. "And you can keep the trophy."

"How kind of you," said Mrs. Friedman.

"This is awesome!" Li cheered. "I can't wait to tell my grandfather."

A judge leaned in. "So what will be the name of the new shelter? Will you name it after Nacho, our hero?"

"Nope. It will be called the Dr. Zhang Animal Shelter," Goldie said.

The winners posed for a few pictures. Goldie insisted that the Gearheads be in several shots.

Zeek stood off to the side with his arms crossed. Goldie could tell that he wasn't waiting around to congratulate her.

"You didn't technically win," he mumbled as she stepped offstage.

"Yeah, we did."

"You tied," Zeek said.

"Tied for a win," Val replied.

"Whatever. I would have won if they hadn't disqualified Ace." Zeek's eyebrows squashed together in an angry V. "You know I can beat you at anything. Anytime."

Goldie rolled her eyes.

"I'd beat you at a science fair, or at a drag race, or in a marathon, or at a cupcake bakeoff."

"Just stop," said Goldie, holding up her hand. "I'm not interested."

But Zeek continued. "I'd win at battle of the bands. Or a race to outer space. Or in an election."

Goldie kept walking. "Let's go celebrate, Gearheads."

Back at the BloxShop, Li, Ruby, and Val ate popcorn and watched old videos of Nacho as a puppy. Goldie tinkered with her machine.

"Aw," Val gushed. "Nacho was the cutest puppy ever."

"Cute, but also destructive," Li said. "He

chewed up one of my helmets and three different sneakers."

"Goldie, what are you working on?" Ruby asked.

"It's the new and improved Commander." Goldie moved the robot in front of the TV.

Nacho jumped off the beanbag and ran toward the door.

"Wait! You have to try it. I think you'll like this one."

Nacho crept toward the new Commander. He pressed the big button with his wet nose. The machine lit up. A backscratcher swung forward and scratched his back. Then a waffle ejected from a slot.

"Listen for the best part," Goldie said.

The Commander spoke. "Nacho, you are the *Best! Pet! Ever!*"